THE GREAT MONSTER CONTEST

BY RUTHANNA LONG

ILLUSTRATED BY GREG AND TIM HILDEBRANDT

GOLDEN PRESS · NEW YORK

Western Publishing Company, Inc.
Racine, Wisconsin

All the forty-eleven monsters in Horrendous Swamp decided to have a contest to choose the champion monster.

That is, all the monsters except one.

2

Her name was Jurgles, and she was much too shy a monster even to dream of parading in a contest.

Besides, there wasn't a chance that she could win. She was sure she couldn't perform in front of a crowd. And she couldn't imagine getting any points for the most talented, most likable, most athletic, or most anything. Every monster she knew was more outstanding at something-or-other than she was.

Scarlotta had scabbier, scalier bumps and much more horrible horns.

Flora DePlora was definitely the prettiest. The sharpest, crunchingest teeth belonged to Dester-Pester, and *Snap!* he had more of them, too.

4

There were smokier monsters
and stronger and faster monsters.
There were bigger and better monsters.

Jurgles was not only shy,
she was discouraged. She sighed
a smoky sigh, and *Splash!*
large tears splashed down her snout
and hit the ground.

Jurgles' best friend, Boomer, who was terribly popular, wobbled over and stood beside her. Together they gazed down into a large puddle of Jurgles' tears.

"I agree with you," Boomer bellowed. "You shouldn't enter the contest."

Boomer batted her enormous, hooded eyes at her own reflection in the puddle at their feet. "I hope I become Miss Congeniality," she confided. "I am well liked, you know."

Clumpety-clump! Clump, clump, clump! Marvin Marvelous skedaddled by on his six legs. When he saw Jurgles and Boomer he skidded to a stop. Marvin was a real wizard at magic tricks and a sure-fire shoo-in for most talented. "Everyone has entered the contest but you, Jurgles," he snorted. "Of course, no one else has a chance with marvelous me in the contest, but I do admire the others for trying."

He blew a cloud of smoke rings and caught them on his horns.

"Jurgles can't win at anything,"
Boomer said. "There's no reason
for her to enter."

Marvin Marvelous stopped to
think. *Zap! Zonk! Pop! Pow! Pow!*
Thinking always made a racket
in Marvin's marvelous head.
"*I* know," he said at last.
"Jurgles will be the judge.
Every contest must have a judge
to count the votes."

So, Jurgles was declared judge
of the Great Monster Contest
to be held in three days at high noon
in Horrendous Swamp.

9

The monsters gathered together and built a judge's stand for Jurgles. They decorated it with bright flowers and pretty stones, and they found a hollow tree trunk on which they put this sign: Vote here for CHAMPION MONSTER.

Everyone was busy.

Some of the more polite monsters made a guest list. They sent invitations to the other creatures they knew — a colony of friendly turtles, a flock of large, noisy birds, and a number of giant dragonflies.

Some of the monsters made posters.

Flora DePlora's poster read, "Vote for me — I'm the prettiest." Other posters proclaimed other good points, but each one ended up with the same message: VOTE FOR ME, ME, ME.

Together the monsters cleared a long runway where the final Great Monster Contest Parade would be held.

Horrendous Swamp certainly did look different.

"I can hardly wait for the great day,"
said Marvin Marvelous. "Look, Jurgles,
now I can blow smoke rings
standing on one leg."

"That's not so much," Dester-Pester shot back,
and he bit a large log in two with one snap.
"I'm sure everyone will vote for me."

The Monster Committee for the Great Monster Contest called all the monsters together, and the chairperson announced the following:

1. First, there will be a picnic to which all our guests are invited.
2. Next, there will be a program. Each contestant will perform.
3. Then, the Grand Parade will take place.
4. After the parade, we will vote for the All-Around Champion Monster. Only monsters can vote.
5. Last, Jurgles will count the votes and announce the winner."

Monsters are not the most agreeable creatures. Some of them wanted the picnic to be last instead of first. Others argued that the guests should be allowed to vote too. There were those who thought *everyone* should count the votes. But at last it was decided to go along with the committee.

Finally, finally, finally, the great day arrived. It started beautifully. The sun shone, there was a pleasant breeze, the sky was as blue as Flora DePlora's eyes, and the clouds were as white as Dester-Pester's teeth.

All of the monsters looked their best. They had
bathed and polished themselves until they positively
gleamed in the sunshine. A few of the vainer ones
were wearing wreaths of flowers and garlands of ferns.

The guests arrived early. A great picnic had been laid out for them under the ginkgoes. There were tasty bamboo sandwiches and scads of young trees to nibble on. Some of the fire-breathing dragons had toasted giant mushrooms, and a swimming monster had made willow branch and water lily salads especially for the guests. Heaps and heaps of fruits and seeds had been gathered, and gallons of cold swampwater lemonade had been made for everyone.

The picnic was a huge success. There was lots of
talking and laughing and chewing and crunching,
and among the monsters, a great deal of loud bragging.

Jurgles took her place on the judge's stand and
made a short speech thanking the Picnic Committee
for all their fine efforts. Then she cleared her throat.
"The talent program will now begin," she said.

"Louder, louder," cried Boomer, motioning for the crowd to be quiet. Boomer decided to take over. She smiled her sweetest smile and boomed, "Attention, friends and guests! The talent program is starting."

Lorenzo the Magnificent was first. He and six of his cousins twisted and turned and stood on their heads and tails until they formed the letters W-E-L-C-O-M-E.

The crowd applauded and cheered.

Scarlotta did a tap dance.

Dester-Pester played a tune on his teeth just as though they were a xylophone,

and Flora DePlora sang a folk song.

Boomer twirled a baton,
which was really a rather
large tree trunk,

and, of course, Marvin Marvelous
blew colored smoke rings,
and squares, and triangles.

27

Then the contestants performed feats of strength and high jumps and broad jumps and tailspins.

A few flying monsters put on an air show, and the swimming monsters did high dives into the nearby lake.

The grand finale was a fireworks display put on
by the fire-breathing monsters.
It was quite a spectacular show.

29

Jurgles then asked all the monsters to form a line for the Grand Parade.

Such commotion! Such crowding and shoving and shouting!

"Me first!"

"I want to be last!"

"You're in *my* place."

"Stop pushing!"

"You stepped on my tail, you clumsy oaf!"

30

"Order, please," Jurgles called. "Please be orderly, please." At long last, after many complaints and much elbowing, the monsters appeared to be ready. Jurgles gave a signal, and the Grand Parade began.

Up and down the runway the monsters marched, bowing and waving and flashing fierce and friendly smiles. Some were show-offs and turned cartwheels or somersaulted, but for the most part they behaved monstrously well.

Jurgles gave the signal for the parade to halt. "Monsters will now take their places and cast their votes. Only one vote apiece, and only monsters can vote," she reminded them.

The guests protested at not being allowed to vote. Some booed and hissed, and a rowdy bunch of young dragonflies and birds decided to boycott the contest. Squawking and flapping their wings, they flew away in disgust. But most of the guests stayed on to wait for the results.

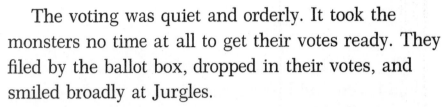

The voting was quiet and orderly. It took the
monsters no time at all to get their votes ready. They
filed by the ballot box, dropped in their votes, and
smiled broadly at Jurgles.

When the last monster had voted, Jurgles began
counting. She counted once, twice, and three times.
Then she counted again.

The crowd waited silently.

Once again Jurgles counted to be absolutely sure.

Slowly she stepped to the edge of the platform.

"I hardly know what to say," she began.

"The results," someone shouted. "We want the results."

"Who came in first?" Lorenzo demanded.

"And second? And third?" others called out.

"Be quiet," Boomer boomed at the crowd. "Give her a chance to tell you."

"Really," Jurgles continued, "it is quite amazing."
She smiled uncertainly. "Nobody wins. It's a tie."
The crowd moved forward toward the judge's stand.
"Of course, there's another way to look at it,"
Jurgles said hastily. "Since everyone got exactly one
vote, everyone wins."

There were angry mutterings and low growls among the monsters in the crowd.

"I demand a recount," Dester-Pester yelled.

"Nonsense," Boomer answered him. "Don't you see what happened?" She was not smiling. "We all voted for ourselves. No one voted for anyone else."

"So it's a tie," added Jurgles,
"and everyone wins."

But the monsters would have
none of that. "How could you
vote for yourself,"
Marvin asked Lorenzo,
"when I was clearly the best?"

"You're selfish and horrible,"
Flora DePlora told Scarlotta.

First there were quarrels.
Then fights broke out.
The guests left as
quickly as they could.
Mad monsters can cause
a lot of damage.

41

The stronger monsters started chasing the weaker monsters. The fire-breathers snorted around and stirred up a great smoke screen. There was coughing and gasping and cries of "I'll show you who's champion," and "Fine friend you are to vote for yourself instead of me."

Jurgles watched with dismay from the judge's stand. Then the smoke became so heavy she could see no more.

The flying monsters flew away to the east, vowing never to return. The swimmers angrily left for another lake. Trees crashed as giant creatures ran after each other into the forest.

Then all was quiet. A faint breeze cleared the last
of the dragon smoke. Jurgles looked all around and
saw that no one — not one single monster — remained.
They had all chased each other away. Even Boomer
was gone. Jurgles called, but there was no answer.
She waited. A chill wind stirred the wilted flowers on
the judge's stand. Dark clouds piled up in the eastern
sky. She waited some more, but no one returned.

It began to rain. Jurgles breathed a long, smoky sigh and watched as it formed a ring. She caught it on her arm and wore it like a bracelet until it blew away. She smiled, thinking of Marvin's trick. Slowly she climbed down from the stand and wandered along the runway. There was no one to watch, so she didn't feel so shy anymore. She did a cartwheel and bowed to the guests who were no longer there.

She swept up a discarded wreath with a flick of her tail and flipped it onto her head.

Now she had come to the edge of the misty lake. As far back as she could remember she had been able to swim, but she had never felt brave enough to try a dive. "I don't think I'm afraid to dive anymore," she said to herself, and she climbed to the top of the cliff. It was lonely there, and very high up, and she wished the other monsters would come back to see how well she could do her tricks. Then she dived into the lake for the first time.

It was a beautiful dive.

Three friendly fish applauded. A group of clams smiled in appreciation.

Jurgles was no longer alone, and she felt right at home in the water. She swam in great circles and dived down, down into the depths. A school of fish and a giant squid swam up to her.

"Here I shall stay," Jurgles said, "until my friends come back."

But the monsters never did return.

And some say that Jurgles still swims in her misty lake, somewhat shy, but quite happy now with her many new friends.